# FIVE GOOFY GHOSTS

by Judith Bauer Stamper
Illustrated by Tim Raglin

**Hello Reader!—Level 4**

SCHOLASTIC INC.
Cartwheel
·B·O·O·K·S·®

New York   Toronto   London   Auckland   Sydney

# A NOTE TO PARENTS

### Reading Aloud with Your Child
*Research shows that reading books aloud is the single most valuable support parents can provide in helping children learn to read.*
- Be a ham! The more enthusiasm you display, the more your child will enjoy the book.
- Run your finger underneath the words as you read to signal that the print carries the story.
- Leave time for examining the illustrations more closely; encourage your child to find things in the pictures.
- Invite your youngster to join in whenever there's a repeated phrase in the text.
- Link up events in the book with similar events in your child's life.
- If your child asks a question, stop and answer it. The book can be a means to learning more about your child's thoughts.

### Listening to Your Child Read Aloud
*The support of your attention and praise is absolutely crucial to your child's continuing efforts to learn to read.*
- If your child is learning to read and asks for a word, give it immediately so that the meaning of the story is not interrupted. DO NOT ask your child to sound out the word.
- On the other hand, if your child initiates the act of sounding out, don't intervene.
- If your child is reading along and makes what is called a miscue, listen for the sense of the miscue. If the word "road" is substituted for the word "street," for instance, no meaning is lost. Don't stop the reading for a correction.
- If the miscue makes no sense (for example, "horse" for "house"), ask your child to reread the sentence because you're not sure you understand what's just been read.
- Above all else, enjoy your child's growing command of print and make sure you give lots of praise. *You are your child's first teacher — and the most important one. Praise from you is critical for further risk-taking and learning.*

— Priscilla Lynch
Ph.D., New York University
Educational Consultant

ISBN 0-590-92152-5

Text copyright © 1996 by Judith Bauer Stamper.
Illustrations copyright © 1996 by Tim Raglin.
All rights reserved. Published by Scholastic Inc.
HELLO READER!, CARTWHEEL BOOKS, and the
CARTWHEEL BOOKS logo are registered trademarks of Scholastic Inc.
The HELLO READER! logo is a trademark of Scholastic Inc.

Library of Congress Cataloging-in-Publication Data

Stamper, Judith Bauer.
    Five goofy ghosts / by Judith Bauer Stamper ; illustrated by Tim Raglin.
        p.    cm. — (Hello reader! Level 4)
    "Cartwheel Books."
    Contents: Never talk to a ghost — A scary tale — The trunk full of treats — The hairy toe — The last laugh.
    ISBN 0-590-92152-5
    1. Ghost stories, American. 2. Humorous stories, American. 3. Children's stories, American. [1. Ghosts — Fiction. 2. Humorous stories. 3. Short stories.] I. Raglin, Tim, ill. II. Title. III. Series.
PZ7.S78612Fk    1996
[E] — dc20                                                                      96-27997
                                                                                    CIP
                                                                                     AC

12 11 10 9 8 7 6 5 4 3 2                                        6 7 8 9/9 0 1/0

Printed in the U.S.A.                                                    23

First Scholastic printing, October 1996

# NEVER TALK TO A GHOST

Late one night, a boy took a walk.

His little dog went with him.

They walked down a lonely, dark lane.


"Wonder if we'll see a ghost?" the boy asked.

His little dog looked at him with big eyes.

They kept on walking down the lane.


The lane made a sharp turn to the left.

Then it came to a stop.

At the end was a big, old house.

"Let's go in," the boy said.
The little dog began to whimper.
He followed the boy to the door.

The old door creaked as it opened.
The boy stepped inside the house.
The dog followed close behind him.

"Anybody home?" the boy called out.
A moan came from up the stairs.
Then the lights went off and on.

"I wonder if it's a ghost?" the boy said.
Just then, the room got colder.
A ghost appeared on the stairs.

"Well, look at that!" the boy said.
The little dog hid behind the boy's legs.
The ghost moaned again.

"Ghosts don't scare me!" the boy said.
The ghost looked angry.
He floated right down the stairs.

"You should be scared!" the ghost said.
The boy started shaking all over.

Fast as he could, the boy ran out the door.
The little dog took off after him.
"I didn't know ghosts could talk," the boy said.

"Me, neither," the dog said. "Let's get out of here!"

# A SCARY TALE

A brother and sister were visiting their grandmother.

She lived in a creepy, old house.

The brother and sister decided to explore.

They climbed up one flight of stairs.
The steps creaked and squeaked.

They climbed up another flight of stairs.
The steps creaked and squeaked.

They climbed up another flight of stairs.
They opened an old door.
It creaked and squeaked.

The brother and sister walked into an old attic.
It was filled with boxes and trunks.
Cobwebs were everywhere.

"This is creepy!" the sister said.
"You're a fraidy-cat," the brother said.
"No, I'm not."
"Yes, you are!"

The sister got mad at her brother.
She wanted to prove that she wasn't a
fraidy-cat.
She looked around and found an old sheet.
She put it over her head.

Then she hid behind a big trunk.
Her brother walked by.
She jumped out and yelled, "Boo!"

Her brother stared at her.
His hair was standing on end.

"It's only me," the sister said.
"I know," her brother said.

"I'm scared of what's behind you!"

# THE TRUNK FULL
# OF TREATS

This is the trunk full of treats.

This is the bat, big and brown,
That's fast asleep, upside down,
Over the trunk full of treats.

This is the skeleton, bony and white,
Waiting in the attic to give you a fright,

If you bother the bat, big and brown,
That's fast asleep, upside down,
Over the trunk full of treats.

This is the witch with long, black hair,
Who rocks all night in her squeaky chair,

Beside the skeleton, bony and white,
Waiting in the attic to give you a fright,
If you bother the bat, big and brown,
That's fast asleep, upside down,
Over the trunk full of treats.

These are the monsters who sit in a bunch,
Moaning and groaning as they munch
and crunch,

Around the witch with long, black hair,
Who rocks all night in her squeaky chair,
Beside the skeleton, bony and white,
Waiting in the attic to give you a fright,
If you bother the bat, big and brown,
That's fast asleep, upside down,
Over the trunk full of treats.

This is the zombie who walks with a thump,
All night you can hear him clumpety-clump.

He guards the monsters who sit in a bunch,
Moaning and groaning as they munch
and crunch,
Around the witch with long, black hair,
Who rocks all night in her squeaky chair,
Beside the skeleton, bony and white,
Waiting in the attic to give you a fright,
If you bother the bat, big and brown,
That's fast asleep, upside down,
Over the trunk full of treats.

This is the ghost who scared the zombie away,

And tickled the monsters and told them to play,

And shooed away the witch on her ragged broom,

And sent the skeleton back to his tomb,

And chased off the bat, big and brown,

And pulled off his sheet and sat himself down,

And opened the trunk full of treats!

# THE HAIRY TOE

Once there was a girl who was very curious.

This girl liked to hunt around for strange things.

In fact, she had a collection of strange things.

She had a snake's skin.

She had a toad's skeleton.

She had a piece of furry moss.

She had lots of other strange things, too.

One day, the girl passed by an old house.
A ghost was supposed to live in this house.
The girl went in anyway, just to look.
And what did she find?
A hairy toe!

"Wow!" the girl said. "A hairy toe for
my collection."
She picked up the hairy toe and ran home.
She set it on the table with her collection.

That night, the girl fell asleep right away.
But a voice woke her in the middle of the night.
"Who-o-o-o's got my hairy toe?"

The girl felt a shiver creep over her.
She pulled her blanket higher over her chin.
Then she heard the voice again, closer.
"Who-o-o-o's got my hairy toe?"

The girl could see the hairy toe on the table.
It seemed to be shining in the moonlight.
Then a cold breeze swept through the room.
And she heard the voice again, louder.
"Who-o-o-o's got my hairy toe?"

A white shape moved across the room.
The girl knew it was the ghost.
She trembled underneath the covers.
The ghost came closer and closer.
"Who-o-o-o's got my hairy toe?"

The girl jumped out of bed and ran for the table.
She picked up the hairy toe.
"Take it!" she yelled.
She threw the hairy toe at the ghost.

The ghost ran away with his hairy toe.
"Oh, goodie!" he said. "I've got my hairy
toe back!"

And the girl never saw him again.

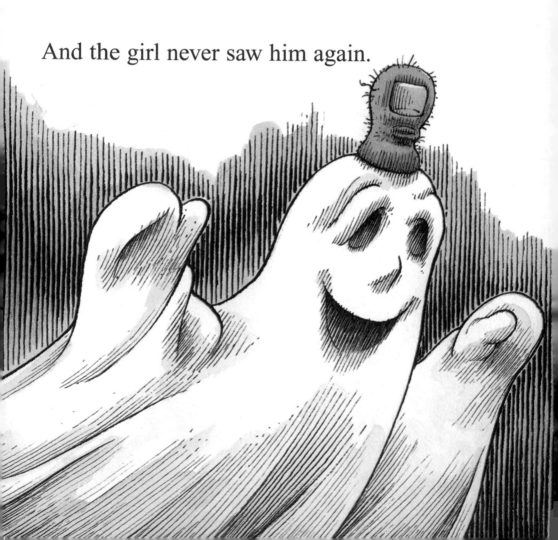

# THE LAST LAUGH

Two boys sat on an old stone wall.
Behind them was a graveyard.

"Do you know what the little ghost wore on
Halloween?" one boy asked.
"A pillowcase."

The boys laughed so hard they almost fell off the wall.

"Where do ghosts go to retire?" the other boy asked.
"A ghost town."

The boys laughed and laughed.

"How did the little ghost do his homework?" the first boy asked.
"He hired a ghostwriter."

The boys laughed so loud their voices echoed in the graveyard.

"Where did the ghost keep his rock collection?" the second boy asked.
"In a graveyard."

The boys laughed and slapped their knees.

"What did the ghost say to the two boys?"
the ghost asked.